The man opened the ..... in the cage so that Holly and her fa... ... could go in. Rusty tilted his head to ... ... them with sparkling ...

Woof? he barked ... ... then trotted up to Holly and nudged her with his damp nose.

"Aw, you're sooooo cute!" Holly cooed, kneeling down and throwing her arms around Rusty. She felt his smooth furry body waggle from nose to tail as she cuddled him.

Mum and Dad had got down on their knees to pet Rusty, too. The little dog's tail had wagged so hard that it became a blur. Baby Adam had stopped wailing and given a gurgle of delight.

"Rusty's the one!" Holly had blurted out.

www.kidsatrandomhouse.co.uk

Have you read all these books in the Battersea Dogs & Cats Home series?

🐾 🐾 🐾 🐾

RUSTY'S
story

by

Jane Clarke

RED FOX

BATTERSEA DOGS & CATS HOME: RUSTY'S STORY
A RED FOX BOOK 978 1 849 41124 0

First published in Great Britain by Red Fox,
an imprint of Random House Children's Books
A Random House Group Company

This edition published 2010

1 3 5 7 9 10 8 6 4 2

The Random House Group Limited supports the Forest Stewardship Council
(FSC), the leading international forest certification organization. All our titles
that are printed on Greenpeace-approved FSC-certified paper carry the FSC
logo. Our paper procurement policy can be found at
www.rbooks.co.uk/environment.

Mixed Sources
Product group from well-managed
forests and other controlled sources
www.fsc.org Cert no. TT-COC-2139
© 1996 Forest Stewardship Council
FSC

Set in 13/20 Stone Informal

Red Fox Books are published by Random House Children's Books,
61–63 Uxbridge Road, London W5 5SA

www.**kids**at**randomhouse**.co.uk
www.**rbooks**.co.uk

Addresses for companies within The Random House Group Limited
can be found at: www.randomhouse.co.uk/offices.htm

THE RANDOM HOUSE GROUP Limited Reg. No. 954009

A CIP catalogue record for this book is available from the British Library.

Printed and bound in Great Britain by
CPI Bookmarque, Croydon, CR0 4TD

Turn to page 99 for lots
of information on the
Battersea Dogs & Cats Home,
plus some cool activities!

Meet the stars of the Battersea Dogs & Cats Home series to date . . .

Bailey

Misty

Chester

Rusty

Max

Daisy

Off to a
Great Start

"Say cheese!" Holly Carter's dad turned round from the driving seat of the car and took a photo with his new digital camera. He handed it to her to look at.

"Perfect!" Holly laughed. In the picture, her eyes were sparkling and there was a huge smile on her freckly face. And no wonder. Sitting on the back seat beside her was the cutest dog in the whole wide

world. Rusty, her
very own dog! He
was sniffing
curiously at
everything with
his rubbery
black nose.

Dad put down
the camera and
started the car.

"Time to go home!" Holly said,
stroking Rusty's velvety ears. She felt as if
her heart would burst with joy.

It felt like ages since Mum and Dad
had promised she could have a dog to
look after when her new baby brother or
sister arrived. The very same day that
Adam was born, Holly had told them
that she wanted to choose her dog from
Battersea Dogs & Cats Home.

"I saw it on TV. They look after dogs that have been lost or abandoned," she'd explained excitedly. "I really want to give one of those dogs a new home and family."

"That's a lovely idea, Holly." Mum smiled as she sat up in the hospital bed cuddling the brand-new baby. "Now, how about saying hello to your baby brother?"

Holly had taken Adam into her arms and gazed down at his crumpled new-baby face.

"Hello, Adam. I'm your big sister, Holly," she'd murmured. "I'm very pleased you're here at last – because now Mum and Dad will let me have my very own dog!"

In the back seat of the car, Rusty yawned and curled up with his head on Holly's lap.

His reddish-brown paws began to twitch
as if he was swimming doggy-paddle in
his sleep. Holly thought she knew what
he was dreaming about.

"It's OK, Rusty," she told him. "You're
safe now." At the sound of her voice, the
little dog relaxed. Becoming a dog
owner's even more exciting than
becoming a big sister! Holly thought.

It had been so
hard to be patient
and wait until Adam
was home and settled
into a routine.

But finally, two weeks ago, just as she was pouring cornflakes into her bowl for breakfast, Dad had announced, "Today we're all going to Battersea Dogs & Cats Home so Holly can choose her dog!"

"Yeeeeeeeeeeeees!" Holly had yelled, jumping into the air, cornflakes flying everywhere.

At the Home, they'd sat down with a
kind man who worked there and he'd
asked them all sorts of questions. Holly
knew the Home needed to be sure they
were serious about becoming dog owners,
but of course baby Adam hadn't
understood and he had begun squalling.

"What kind of dog are you looking
for?" the man asked Holly, raising his
voice so she could hear him.

"A nice friendly little dog," Holly told him. "It really doesn't matter what breed. I just want to help a dog to find a happy home."

The man had smiled. "In that case," he said, "I'd like you to meet Rusty. He's a terrier cross, under a year old."

Still a puppy, really! Holly thought.

"He was very shy when he first came to us," the man went on, "but now Rusty's one of the friendliest dogs I've ever looked after. The fire brigade brought him to us. You'll never guess where they found him . . ."

Love at
First Sight

Holly still found it hard to believe what
the man in the Home had told them on
that very first day. She frowned a little,
remembering.

"Someone spotted Rusty in the middle
of the river Thames and called the fire
brigade to rescue him!" the man said as
he led Holly and her family to the
kennels. "In central London! We think

someone threw him into the water . . ."

Holly looked at her mum and dad. Their mouths had dropped open.

"How could anyone do that?" Holly said, shocked. She'd been on a London boat trip on the muddy-looking Thames. "It's really, really deep! He could have drowned!"

"Luckily Rusty's a really good swimmer," the man said, stopping outside a cage. A little dog with short hair that gleamed brighter than Holly's grandma's copper kettle trotted up to the bars, wagging his tail. "Rusty was exhausted, but he was still doing the doggy paddle when they found him," the man went on.

"Poor, poor Rusty," Holly said. She could hardly bear to think of such a sweet little dog struggling in the huge fast-flowing muddy river.

"It must have been a horrible experience," the man agreed. "And it's taken a while for Rusty to get over his mistrust of people. But he's fine now, as you can see. I'll be sorry to see him go, but he deserves to be part of a happy home." He opened the door to the cage so that Holly and her family could go in.

Rusty tilted his head to one side and gazed at them with sparkling brown eyes.

Woof? he barked
enquiringly,
then he trotted
up to Holly
and nudged
her with his
damp nose.

"Aw, you're
sooooo cute!"
Holly cooed,
kneeling down
and throwing her
arms around Rusty. She
felt his smooth furry body waggle from
nose to tail as she cuddled him.

Mum and Dad had got down on their
knees to pet Rusty, too. The little dog's tail
had wagged so hard that it became a
blur. Baby Adam had stopped wailing
and given a gurgle of delight.

"Rusty's the one!" Holly had blurted out.

Holly's dad got out his new camera and took a photo of them all right there and then.

The man from the Home had looked really pleased. "I can see that Rusty will get on with everyone," he'd told them. "Within the next week to ten days, we'll arrange for someone from the Home to come and visit your house to make sure that Rusty will be happy there. After that, we'll give him a health check and fit him with a microchip . . ."

"What's that?" Holly asked.

"A microchip is a small pellet, the size of a grain of rice," the man explained. "It will be injected into the scruff of Rusty's neck."

Holly made a face.

"It's quite painless, and he won't notice it's there," the man reassured her. "The chip is programmed with a number and it can be read with a barcode scanner."

"Like in the supermarket?" Holly asked. "Cool!"

"That's right," the man told her. "The number on it will be registered and linked to your home address and telephone

number, so if Rusty ever gets lost, the
Home or a vet or the police can scan him
and find out who he belongs to."

"And once Rusty's had his health
check and microchip . . . ?" Holly had
asked eagerly. "What happens then?"

The man smiled. "Then you can come
and collect him and take him home for
good . . ."

"Yaaay!" she'd
cheered.

Beside Holly on the car seat, Rusty's ears pricked up. He had a little patch of white fur on the side of each ear. How could anyone ever have abandoned him? Holly wondered, watching him yawn and stretch. He's the cutest dog ever!

Rusty sat up and pressed his nose to the car window, leaving a big smudgy mark.

"We're home!" Dad said, leaping out of the car with the camera. "I'll get a photo of Rusty's arrival."

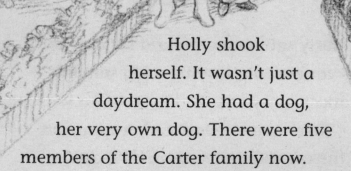

Holly shook
herself. It wasn't just a
daydream. She had a dog,
her very own dog. There were five
members of the Carter family now.

Rusty the Waterhound

Rusty slowly sniffed his way through the hall and living room into the kitchen.

"He's sussing us out." Holly grinned, opening the door into the utility room.

Rusty looked up and wagged his tail.

Click! Dad took a photo.

"You sleep here, Rusty," Holly said, patting the padded dog basket covered with a gold-and-brown paw-print design. Rusty sniffed suspiciously at it.

"It's really comfy, look." Holly threw herself into it.

Click! went the camera.

"And this is your water bowl." Holly pointed to a big stainless-steel bowl brimful of water.

Rusty stepped carefully into the bowl. He stood there wagging his tail, with a big doggy grin on his face.

Click!

"He thinks it's a paddling pool," Holly giggled.

She opened the back door. Mum was out there, unpegging baby clothes from the washing line and dropping them into the basket at her feet. Adam was lying on his baby mat next to her, happily kicking his feet in the early evening sunshine.

"Welcome to the garden, Rusty," Mum called.

"You'll love it out here!" Holly encouraged him.

Rusty cautiously trotted out into the garden. Then, suddenly, he froze. He lifted his muzzle and sniffed deeply, whiffling his long whiskers.

Woooooof! he barked in delight, breaking into a trot.

"Mind the goldfish pond!" Holly called.

Too late.

Rusty fell into the pond with a *splash!*

An image of Rusty paddling for his life
in the river Thames flashed through
Holly's mind. He'll be terrified, she
thought as she raced to his rescue.

But there was no need to worry.
Rusty was doing the doggy
paddle in circles around
the little pond, clearly
loving every splashy
second.

"One bad experience hasn't put him off water," Dad laughed, taking another photo as Rusty hauled himself out of the pond. "Watch out! He's going to shake!"

"Yeerk!" Holly squealed as cold water droplets sprayed all down her legs.

"Mind us!" Mum yelled, scooping up Adam and dumping him on top of the washing basket. She ran indoors with it as Rusty shook himself from nose to tail.

Waaah! Adam yelled. Rusty stopped shaking himself dry and looked at Holly enquiringly.

"Don't worry, babies do that a lot," Holly told Rusty as Mum reappeared with Adam. She stretched out her arms for her little brother. Then she carefully held Adam so that he could see Rusty and Rusty could see him. Rusty wagged his tail. Instantly, Adam stopped crying and began to smile.

He stretched out his hand. Holly knelt down so that Adam could stroke Rusty's damp head with his podgy baby fingers.

"You two are going to be great friends," Holly told them with a grin.

"I'm sure they will be," said Dad. "But Adam's just a little baby, so you must make sure he's never left alone with Rusty, in case Rusty gets a bit boisterous and hurts him accidentally."

"More like in case Adam gets a bit boisterous with Rusty!" Holly muttered, untangling Adam's fingers from Rusty's ear.

"Rusty is *my* dog, Adam," Holly told her little brother. "You can play with him, but only when I'm supervising!"

Gooo! Adam gurgled as Holly handed him back to Mum.

"I'm glad you understand," Holly giggled. She grabbed an old towel and gently rubbed Rusty's coat until he was soft, dry and gleaming.

Mum smiled and looked at her watch. "It's Adam's bath time!" she announced, carrying Adam towards the stairs. Dad settled down on the settee and opened his newspaper.

"It can't be that time already!" Holly said in amazement. The day was flying by. "Stay here, Rusty." She patted the floor at Dad's feet.

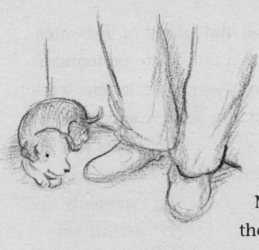

"I'll be
down
to play
just as
soon as
I've helped
Mum give
the baby his
bath." Rusty lay down and put his head
on his paws. Holly noticed his ears prick
up when he heard the sound of water
running into the
bath.

Adam
loves water
as much as
Rusty, Holly
thought, watching her
baby brother gurgle with delight as he
splashed in the warm bubbly water.

She was pretending a rubber duck was nibbling at his toes when suddenly the bathroom door swung open. Holly looked up. A red-brown shadow hurled itself towards the bath.

"Rusty!" she shrieked, dropping the yellow duck.

Just in time, Mum grabbed Adam. Rusty landed in the soapy water.

Splosh!

A wave broke over the top of the bath and sloshed onto the floor. Rusty stood in the nearly-empty bath, wagging his tail. He was covered in bubbles.

I really should tell him off, Holly thought, but she was giggling too much to say anything.

"Take him outside before he shakes himself!" Mum spluttered.

Holly hauled her damp dog out of the bath and hurried him downstairs, leaving a trail of bubbles and wet paw prints. She opened the back door.

Rusty paused for a second . . . then launched himself into the pond. His little legs were a blur in the water as he doggy-paddled round and round.

Mum appeared
beside her with
Adam wrapped in
a towel.

Gooo! he
gurgled, pointing
and smiling at
Rusty.

"Sorry, Adam,
Rusty's not allowed
to join you at bath
time!" Mum said. Holly could tell she
wasn't too cross really.

"Rusty just loves water!" Holly
laughed, grabbing a towel. "He's a real
waterhound!"

A Big Surprise

"Rusty's been here a week and he's settled down really well," Dad said on Sunday morning as the Carter family sat round the breakfast table. "It's time to make some holiday plans. We thought we'd take the ferry to France next month—"

"But dogs can't go to France, can they?" Holly frowned. "We can't leave

Rusty behind! He'll think he's been abandoned again. I'll stay at home and look after him."

"Rusty can come with us if we get him a pet passport," Dad said. "We've added Adam to your mum's and my passports, but Rusty has to have his own."

"What, like mine?" Holly was very proud that she had her own passport.

"Very like it," Dad said, "but it's a bit more complicated for dogs. I've made an appointment for him at the vet's after school tomorrow."

The vet's? Holly thought. Her tummy did a somersault.

"Is something wrong with Rusty?" she asked worriedly.

"Rusty's fine. He had his health check at the Home, remember? He has to see the vet, because the vet is the person who will issue Rusty with his pet passport," Dad explained.

"He'll need a picture!" Holly said, remembering her own passport photo being taken at the chemist's. "Is he allowed to smile?"

"You can choose any picture you want." Dad grinned. "There are lots on my camera."

"Brilliant!" said Holly, running off to get it. She scrolled through the pictures . . . "Rusty jumping in the pond . . ." she murmured. "Rusty doing doggy paddle . . . Aw! This one's the cutest!" She showed Mum and Dad the picture she had taken of Rusty sitting next to his water bowl.

She couldn't wait for Rusty to get his passport. Taking him to France was going to be such fun!

Next day, after school, Holly, Mum and Adam took Rusty to the vet's. He sat patiently next to them in the waiting room until his name was called, and he wagged his tail when a lady plonked a cat in an animal carrier on the floor beside him.

"What a friendly little dog." The lady cat owner smiled. Holly felt as if she would burst with pride.

"Now, what can we do for this little fellow?" the vet asked.

"Rusty needs a pet passport," Holly said excitedly. "I've got his picture right here!"

"Great photo." The vet smiled. "Does Rusty have a microchip?"

Holly nodded.

"Then first I need to scan that." The vet took out something that looked like a cross between a TV remote control and a calculator and gently swiped it along the left side of Rusty's neck.

Beep!

The vet showed the machine to Holly. "That's Rusty's microchip number," she said, pointing to a line of numbers,

which she
wrote
down on a
form. Even though it
was upside down from
where she was standing,
Holly could make out the
words *Pet Passport* on it.

"Now for his rabies vaccination."
The vet opened her refrigerator and took
out a little box with a tiny bottle in it.
She filled a syringe with the contents of
the bottle.

Holly tried not to shudder. I mustn't show Rusty I don't like injections, she thought. Adam took one look at the needle and began to wail. Mum bounced him up and down in the baby carrier, trying to comfort him.

Holly patted Rusty's head as the vet gathered up a handful of loose skin at the back of his neck, and gave him the injection. Rusty wagged his tail.

Holly breathed
a sigh of relief.
"He didn't feel
that at all!"
she exclaimed.

"Bring him back in three weeks for a
blood test to make sure the rabies
vaccination worked," the vet told them.
"If it has, I'll issue him with a passport."

"That'll just be in time for our holiday
in France!" Holly said happily.

"Don't forget, you
have to wait six
months from the date
the blood sample was
taken before you
can come
back into the
UK," the vet
warned them.

"But that means we won't be able to bring Rusty back home until after Christmas!" Holly gasped. "We'll have to stay in France!"

"There's no way we can stay that long!" Mum exclaimed, raising her voice to be heard above Adam's crying. "Rusty's not going to be able to come on holiday to France with us, I'm afraid. But I'm sure he will be happy in the kennels."

Holly's heart felt as
if it had plummeted
onto the floor of the
vet's surgery. Tears
started to spurt
out of her eyes
and trickle down
her cheeks.

"If Rusty can't go to
France, I'm not going either!" she wailed.

Change of Plan

Holly was still sobbing on Rusty's neck when Dad came home. Mum explained the situation to him in the kitchen. After a while Dad came into the living room.

"I didn't realize it would take so long to get a pet passport," Dad said. "Don't worry, you don't have to go on holiday without Rusty."

"I don't?" Holly sniffed.

"We haven't booked a ferry or a cottage in France," Dad explained, "so we can change our plans. We'll go to France next year when Rusty has his passport."

"Thanks, Dad." Holly smiled a watery smile.

"And," Dad said, with a twinkle in his eye, "we can still go on a ferry this year, without leaving the country!"

"How?" Holly asked incredulously as Mum came into the room, carrying Adam.

"We're going to the Isle of Wight!" Mum and Dad said together.

"Yeeeeeeees!" Holly yelled, hugging Rusty. She had the best dog and Mum and Dad and baby brother in the whole wide world!

Holly dashed upstairs, with Rusty racing after her, and pulled her pink suitcase out of the bottom of her wardrobe. She could hardly wait!

Mum stuck her head round the door. "We're not going for another three weeks," she laughed as Holly stuffed in her swimming costume and towel.

At last it was the night before their holiday. Holly was wide awake. There was no way she could sleep. She crept out of bed and tiptoed downstairs, past Mum and Dad, who were watching TV,

and out into the utility room. Rusty
raised his head and thumped his tail as
she crawled into his basket.

"We're going on holiday
tomorrow," she
told him,
snuggling
up to his
warm
furry body.
"You'll love
it! We're
going to a
beach where dogs
are allowed, and you'll get to swim in the
sea! That's much nicer than the goldfish
pond. And there will be lots of crabs to
sniff at. Well . . . maybe that's not such a
good idea, but you can sniff at shells and
seaweed and . . ."

Holly's voice tailed off as her eyelids began to close.

"Back to bed, Holly." Mum's whisper woke her as she was carried upstairs. "The sooner you go to sleep properly the sooner tomorrow will come!"

It was time to go!

Holly was sitting in the middle of the back seat of the car with Adam strapped in his baby seat on one side of her, and Rusty on the other. She leaned across and opened the window on Rusty's side a few centimetres.

Slurp! His long pink tongue licked her on the cheek.

"Yuk!" Holly giggled, wiping off the doggy drool with the back of her hand.

"Where's my camera when I need it?" Dad laughed.

"Safely packed in the suitcase," Mum told him as he backed out of their driveway. Soon they were on the road leaving town. Rusty stuck his nose out of the window, sniffing the air. The wind made his ears flap.

"Don't let him stick his whole head out," Mum warned. "He might get hit by something."

As they got closer and closer to Southampton, Rusty's sniffs got deeper and deeper. He began to shift around on the seat.

"He can smell the sea!" Holly said. She could, too. It smelled of journeys and holidays and excitement!

Dad drove into the ferry port and they queued for the ticket check.

"You must leave your dog in the car for the duration of the crossing," the lady at the booth told them.

"Awww!" Holly groaned.

"Rusty will be fine in the car," Dad said, pulling up and parking in a lane of cars that were waiting to get on the boat. "It isn't a long crossing. And we don't want a dog-overboard situation, do we?"

"Or a wet-patch-on-the-back-seat situation!" Holly said. "I'll let Rusty out."

She clipped on Rusty's lead and led him to a grassy area with a fence around it. A boy was there, throwing a ball to a dog that looked like a Labrador cross.

Holly unclipped Rusty's lead. He lifted his leg on the gatepost, then trotted towards the other dog, wagging his tail.

"His name's
Archie," the boy said,
"and I'm Tom. I'm
nine. How old are you?"

"I'm nine, too!"
Holly said as Rusty
chased after Archie.
"My dog's called Rusty.
He's from Battersea
Dogs & Cats Home."

"Archie's from a rescue centre as
well!" Tom said. He tipped some water
out of a bottle into a
water bowl and
held it out to
Archie. "We got
him last year.

How long have you had Rusty?"

"A whole month!" Holly said as Rusty took a big slurp from Archie's bowl. "He's my very best friend."

"Archie's mine too!" Tom said with a grin.

"Please return to your vehicles!" a voice announced from a loudspeaker. "The Isle of Wight ferry is ready to load."

Holiday Magic

It was a very smooth crossing. Holly
stood on the ferry deck and leaned on the
rail, watching the deep blue sea roll past.
I'm glad Rusty's safe in the car, she
thought. We'd never find him if he
jumped off a ferry!

In what seemed like no time at all
they had reached the island, and Holly
raced back to the car deck. Rusty blinked

up at her
when she
opened the
door, and
thumped his
tail on the
seat.

"He's been
very good in
the back of
the car," Holly told Mum and Dad.
"I think he's been fast asleep the whole
time. He deserves an ice cream! A big soft
swirly one . . ."

"You mean *you'd* like an ice cream,"
Dad laughed. "We'll get one when we
stop in the village to pick up the key from
Holiday Homes."

Right next to the Holiday Homes
office there was a van selling the sort of

ice cream Holly liked. She had just enough time to queue up and get one before Dad got back.

"Eat it in the car," he told her. "I want to find the cottage!"

Rusty looked curiously at Holly as she licked her yummy ice cream. A string of doggy drool dripped onto his paw. Holly broke off the bottom of the cornet and filled it with ice cream. She held it out to him.

Rusty lapped at it, wagging his tail. Soon Holly's fingers were all slobbery.

"You should make it last longer that that!" Holly said as he crunched up the cornet. "Dad's holiday rule is only one ice cream a day!"

Rusty licked his lips.

"This must be it!" Dad pulled the car up beside a row of blue and white

painted holiday cottages. Their cottage
door opened onto the beach, and the
beach sloped down to the sea! It was
awesome! Holly couldn't wait to get out
of the car, and nor could Rusty.

Woof! Woof! Woof! he barked, racing
towards the water with Holly close
behind.

Splish, splosh, splash! He dashed into
the sparkling blue sea.

He stood there for a moment, licking his lips. Gentle waves lapped around his legs.

He's never seen the sea before, Holly thought as she bent down to rinse her slobbery fingers in the warm water. "It doesn't taste like the goldfish pond, does it, Rusty?"

Rusty gave another joyous bark and began to doggy-paddle in the shallows.

The rest of the family joined Holly at the water's edge.

"Rusty thinks this is a great place for a holiday!" Holly told them. "He's having fun already!"

Suddenly Rusty gave a great *woof!* and raced out of the water. Holly looked up. A boy eating an ice cream and carrying a bucket and spade was walking along the beach towards them. Next to him, gazing up longingly at his dripping ice cream, was a familiar-looking Labrador-like dog.

"Tom! what are you doing here?" Holly exclaimed as Rusty gambolled up to Archie.

"We just got here! We're in a cottage a couple of doors down," Tom said, in between licks. "Hey, maybe we could hang out a bit together. My two big sisters just want to spend the week lying around on the sand." He bent down to share the end of his ice-cream cone with Archie and Rusty. "Today I'm going to make a ginormous sandcastle. Want to join in?

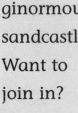

Archie's good at digging, he can teach Rusty!"

Rusty looked up at Holly with puppy-dog eyes.

Holly looked up at her mum and dad with puppy-dog eyes, too. "Pleeeease?" she said.

Mum and Dad burst out laughing.

"Go on," Mum told her. "You can unpack later."

"This is the best holiday ever!" Holly told
her mum and dad that evening when
they came to kiss her goodnight. From
her room, she could hear Rusty and
Adam's contented snores and peer
through the window and watch the
moonlit waves break against the
ramparts of the huge sandcastle she and
Rusty had made with their new friends,
Tom and
Archie.

"This place
is magic!" she
declared.

In Deep Trouble

"It's time for Adam's nap," Mum said after lunch next day. "Dad will stay here while I nip out to the shops. Stay close to the cottage, Holly, and don't go into the sea unless one of us is about. The waves are rough this afternoon."

"Don't worry, Mum," Holly said. "Tom and Archie will be along soon. OK if we go to the adventure playground behind the cottages?"

"As long as you all go together." Mum raised her voice so she could be heard over the grizzling baby. "See you later." She grabbed the car keys, and Dad disappeared upstairs with Adam.

On the beach, the high tide was eating into the sandcastle Holly and Tom had made yesterday. Holly stood and watched a big wave wash the last of it away.

There was
still no sign
of Tom or Archie.
Holly took a tennis
ball out of the pocket of
her shorts.

"It's just you and me
for now, Rusty," she told
him, tossing him a tennis ball.
"Catch!"

Rusty leaped into
the air and
grabbed the ball.

"Good boy!
Now bring it
back."

Rusty dropped
the ball and
began to sniff at a
piece of seaweed.

"Fetch, Rusty!" Holly yelled. "Bring the ball back!"

Rusty turned his back and trotted off down the beach, merrily sniffing the sand.

"I think we need to work on *fetch*!" Holly murmured. The ball was rolling down the beach towards the choppy sea. She skidded down the slope and bent to grab it before it was swept away.

Swooosh!

An enormous wave broke over her head, knocking her off her feet.

"Oof!" she gasped, struggling to stand up. But before she could get her balance back, a second wave knocked her flat with a great *SLAP!*

She held her breath as the wave's undertow tumbled and tossed her out to sea.

It was like being in a giant washing machine! Holly thought her lungs would burst and she'd be lost for ever in the wave's dark blue-green depths. She kicked wildly towards the lighter water at the surface.

Phew! She was out of the wave! Holly trod water, gasping and spluttering. Her eyes were half blinded by the stinging salt water and she could feel a strong ocean current whirling around her legs.

Don't panic, she told herself. You're a good swimmer and you're not far off the beach.

She struck out for the shore, but the current was too strong for her to swim against in her sodden T-shirt and shorts. Tears sprang to her eyes.

You're not going to drown, Holly told herself, blinking away the tears. Some of the sea salt cleared from her eyes.

She could make out Tom and Archie coming along the beach!

"Help!"she called. "Heeeelp!" but her mouth filled with nasty salty water every time she opened it.

They can't hear me! she thought despairingly as she tried desperately to tread water and wave. I'm really in trouble now!

Rusty to
the Rescue

WOOF!

Even though it was muffled by the
noise of the waves, Holly recognized the
bark. Her heart leaped.

Rusty!

He'd seen her! He was darting
backwards and forwards, barking at the
sea. But Tom still hadn't noticed anything
was wrong! He was wandering along the

beach licking an ice cream and Archie
had his eyes fixed on that. Holly watched
them stop at her holiday cottage, look
along the beach, then turn back the way
they had come.

"I'm here, I'm here," Holly whimpered.
It felt like all the strength had drained out
of her and she was being dragged down.

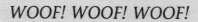

WOOF! WOOF! WOOF!
The sound of Rusty's
bark sent hope surging
through her.

Rusty was running
up to Tom and
Archie! He stood
right in front of
them, barking
furiously, then
turned and dashed into the sea. He was
swimming steadily
towards her!

Holly
blinked
her sore
eyes and
peered
towards
the beach.

Archie and Tom were rushing to the water's edge. Archie's ears pricked up as he barked after Rusty. Tom stood with his hand over his eyes, squinting out over the waves.

"Heeelp!" Holly tried to yell again. She gagged as her mouth filled with sea water. She waved frantically.

Tom waved back!

Yes! Holly thought. Rusty did it! Tom's seen me at last!

Tom and Archie turned
and raced towards her
parents' cottage. They're
going to fetch help!
Holly thought. She
breathed a sigh of relief.

Slurp! Something gave her cheek a big lick.

"Rusty!" Holly gasped. He was bobbing up and down in the water, as steady and reassuring as a life raft. She could feel him grab the neck of her T-shirt in his teeth and begin to doggy-paddle back to the beach. Holly lay on her back and kicked her legs as hard as she could.

Rusty pulled her into the shallows.
There was sand beneath her feet again!
She was safe! Holly staggered up the
beach and sat there, exhausted, spitting
out sea water and catching her breath.
Rusty shook himself from nose to tail,
then sat down beside her, nudging her
gently with his rubbery nose. Holly
stroked his damp ears.

"Thanks!" she
whispered.

"Holly! Are
you OK?" Dad
came flying
out of the
holiday cottage
with Adam in his
arms, closely
followed by Tom, just as
the car drew up with Mum in it. She
leaped out of the car and raced to the
water's edge.

"I'm fine," Holly told her dad as he put a big fluffy towel around her shaking shoulders. "Rusty fished me out, just like the fire brigade fished him out of the river Thames!"

"That's awesome!" Tom said, patting Rusty on the head. "Your rescue dog rescued you!"

"And Tom and Archie helped, too," Holly said. "They are all heroes!"

"Goo!" Adam agreed.

"I think everyone deserves an enormous ice cream," Mum said, hugging Holly in relief. "At least, everyone but Holly. I told you not to go into the sea, remember?!"

"Sorry, Mum," Holly said. "I'll never ever do that again. But I really really need an ice cream to get the taste of salt water out of my mouth. Pleeeease!"

Holly, Rusty, Tom and Archie looked up with puppy-dog eyes.

"OK, OK!" Mum laughed. "That makes six enormous soft ice creams, plus a tiny one for Adam!"

Holly was feeling fine now. "Rusty still likes swimming, so I won't let this put me off swimming, either!" she told Tom and Rusty and Archie as they waited for the ice creams to arrive. "We'll have lots of fun in the sea together for the rest of the holiday!"

Wooooof! Rusty barked.

Woof! Archie echoed.

"I agree!" Tom grinned.

Dad set up the camera on a flat rock
to take a photo of them all sitting on the
beach licking their ice creams.

Click!

He held out the camera
for Holly to see.

"Perfect!" she laughed. Both she and
Tom were clutching two ice creams,
licking one and holding out the other for
their doggy best friends to lick.

"Photos capture great memories."
Mum smiled.

Holly threw her arms around Rusty's
damp shoulders as he munched every
last morsel of his ice-cream cone. "I'm
never ever going to forget my first
holiday with my brave rescue dog!" she
said, giving him an enormous hug.

Rusty's tail wagged and wagged and
wagged.

Battersea Dogs & Cats Home

Battersea Dogs & Cats Home is a charity that aims never to turn away a dog or cat in need of our help. We reunite lost dogs and cats with their owners; when we can't do this, we care for them until new homes can be found for them; and we educate the public about responsible pet ownership. Every year the Home takes in around 12,000 dogs and cats. In addition to the site in south-west London, the Home also has two other centres based at Old Windsor, Berkshire, and Brands Hatch, Kent.

The original site in Holloway

History

The Temporary Home for Lost and Starving Dogs was originally opened in a stable yard in Holloway in 1860 by Mary Tealby after she found a starving puppy in the street. There was no one to look after him, so she took him home and nursed him back to health. She was so worried about the other dogs wandering the streets that she opened the Temporary Home for Lost and Starving Dogs. The Home was established to help to look after them all and find them new homes.

Sadly Mary Tealby died in 1865, aged sixty-four, and little more is known about her, but her good work was continued. In 1871 the Home moved to its present site in Battersea, and was renamed the Dogs' Home Battersea.

Some important dates for the Home:

1883 – Battersea start taking in cats.

1914 – 100 sledge dogs are housed at the Hackbridge site, in preparation for Ernest Shackleton's second Antarctic expedition.

1956 – Queen Elizabeth II becomes patron of the Home.

2004 – Red the Lurcher's night-time antics become world famous when he is caught on camera regularly escaping from his kennel and liberating his canine chums for midnight feasts.

2007 – The BBC broadcast *Animal Rescue Live* from the Home for three weeks from mid-July to early August.

The process for re-homing a dog or a cat

When a lost dog or cat arrives, Battersea's Lost Dogs & Cats Line works hard to try to find the animal's owners. If, after seven days, they have not been able to reunite them, the search for a new home can begin.

The Home works hard to find caring, permanent new homes for all the lost and unwanted dogs and cats.

Dogs and cats have their own characters and so staff at the Home will spend time getting to know every dog and cat. This helps decide the type of home the dog or cat needs.

There are five stages of the re-homing process at Battersea Dogs & Cats Home. Battersea's re-homing team wants to find you the perfect pet, sometimes this can take a while, so please be patient while we search for your new friend!

1 Application

2 Interview

3 Home visit

4 Searching for a pet

5 Leaving with your new pet

Have a look at our website:
http://www.battersea.org.uk/dogs/ rehoming/index.html for more details!

Dos and Don'ts of looking after dogs and cats

Dogs dos and don'ts

DO

- Be gentle and quiet around dogs at all times – treat them how you would like to be treated.
- Have respect for dogs.

DON'T

- Sneak up on a dog – you could scare them.
- Tease a dog – it's not fair.
- Stare at a dog – dogs can find this scary.
- Disturb a dog who is sleeping or eating.

- Assume a dog wants to play with you. Just like you, sometimes they may want to be left alone.
- Approach a dog who is without an owner as you won't know if the dog is friendly or not.

Cats dos and don'ts

DO
- Be gentle and quiet around cats at all times.
- Have respect for cats.
- Let a cat approach you in their own time.

DON'T
- Never stare at a cat as they can find this intimidating.

- Tease a cat – it's not fair.
- Disturb a sleeping or eating cat – they may not want attention or to play.
- Assume a cat will always want to play. Like you, sometimes they want to be left alone.

Here is a delicious recipe for you to follow.

Remember to ask an adult to help you.

Cheddar Cheese Dog Cookies

You will need:

227g grated Cheddar cheese

(use at room temperature)

114g margarine

1 egg

1 clove of garlic (crushed)

172g wholewheat flour

30g wheatgerm

1 teaspoon salt

30ml milk

Preheat the oven to 375°F/190°C/gas mark 5.

Cream the cheese and margarine together.
When smooth, add the egg and garlic and

mix well. Add the flour, wheatgerm and salt. Mix well until a dough forms.Add the milk and mix again.

Chill the mixture in the fridge for one hour.

Roll the dough onto a floured surface until it is about 4cm thick. Use cookie cutters to cut out shapes.

Bake on an ungreased baking tray for 15–18 minutes.

Cool to room temperature and store in an airtight container in the fridge.

Some fun pet-themed puzzles!

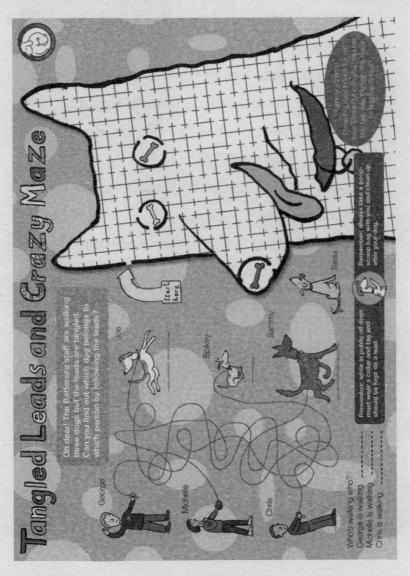

Here is a list of things that you need to think about before getting a dog. See if you can find them in the word search and while you look, think why they might be so important. Only look for words written in blue. They can be written backwards, diagonally, forwards, up and down so look carefully and GOOD LUCK!

SIZE
MALE OR FEMALE
AGE
COAT TYPE
COST
BEHAVIOUR
BASIC TRAINING
HOUSE TRAINING
TIME ALONE
GOOD WITH: PETS, CHILDREN,
STRANGERS, DOGS.
HOW: ENERGETIC, CUDDLY,
STRONG WILLED, INDEPENDENT

Remember: when training a dog, reward works better than punishment.

Can you think of any other things? Write them in the spaces below.

112